4/22/17

To Vyas & Dheeksha,

to my favorite neigh

with love from

Auntie Sue +

Biscuit

AuthorHouse™
1663 Liberty Drive
Bloomington, IN 47403
www.authorhouse.com
Phone: 1 (800) 839-8640

In the event author, Norma Slavit, is not available Joel Slavit will
act in her behalf for any business pertaining to this book.

Published by AuthorHouse 10/29/2015

ISBN: 978-1-5049-5293-4 (sc)
ISBN: 978-1-5049-5334-4 (e)

Library of Congress Control Number: 2015917605

Print information available on the last page.

This book is printed on acid-free paper.

authorHOUSE®

PEACHES, FROG and the MAN IN THE MOON

Written by Norma Slavit

Illustrations by Emily Prough

Note to the parent and teacher:

This picture book, for the four-seven year old, stretches the child's imagination and is designed to engage, entertain and delight young minds.

Repetitive phrases and humorous rhymes help develop the child's ear for speech and reading.

A subtle reference to nutritional foods is woven into the text, and a spirit of cooperation and team effort is emphasized as each animal makes a contribution to the moon trip.

The playful polka dot frog learns that patience often brings rewards.

This book highlights a number readiness sequence and includes an educational supplement.

BOOK DEDICATION

To my precious grandchildren ... Ilana, Rachel, and Joshua

To my grandchildren's dear parents ...Joel, Betsy, Lisa and Steve

To the memory of my beloved parents ...Rose and Max

And to the blessed memory of my dear husband... Herb

SPECIAL ACKNOWLEDGEMENTS

A special "thank you" to Luanna Leisure, author of three books, for her help and assistance.

Thanks to Steve Barkin for his expert technical support.

A note of appreciation to my fiancée, Paul Staschower, for his love and patience.

Preface

Once upon a time when all the animals were friendly, they knew how to talk to each other. That was long ago before they grunted, growled, squeaked or squawked. One day, in the remote forest where they lived, an unmanned spaceship seemed to fall from the sky. Peaches, the friendly baboon, and his friend the polka dot frog watched the spaceship streak across the sky. It made a perfect landing.

With the polka dot frog perched on his shoulder, Peaches swung from tree to tree through the thick forest until they located the spaceship.

"This is the spot," Peaches told frog. They dropped down from one limb to another, finally reaching the bottom.

"I am the only animal who knows how to fly a spaceship like this," Peaches boasted as they inspected the spaceship cabin. "Many years ago when astronauts took animals into space I watched carefully and learned how to fly."

"Well then, my friend," said frog. "Let's take off right now."

"Not so fast," replied Peaches. "First, we must come up with a plan.

Then we need to find someone to help us."

"What's the plan?" frog asked.

"Who will help us?"

"Be patient," replied Peaches.

"Where will we go?

And when can we leave?" asked frog replying as fast as a frog knows how to jump high.

"I don't have all the answers yet, but when I do, I will tell you.

Be patient," encouraged Peaches.

“Be patient?” asked frog,

“What does that mean?”

Peaches and the polka dot frog

fell asleep on a moss-covered log.

As they slept . . . . .

Zillions of twinkling fireflies

Lit up the forest velvet skies.

Sent by the moon on a spiral beam,

Peaches knew this was no dream.

Fireflies delivered an invitation.

It woke up Peaches' imagination.

The friendly baboon turned the invitation over and over in the smooth palms of his thick, hairy hands. Then he read it to frog.

"Now I can tell you ***where*** we are going," said Peaches.

"We are going to the *moon*."

“TO THE MOON,” sang frog, doing a cartwheel dance.

“Can we leave now?” asked frog. “The poor man in the moon must be so lonely.”

“Not so fast, my friend. First, I have to see if my plan works.”

“Who wants to fly to the moon?” Peaches called out.

Peaches and frog waited for someone to come.

No one came.

Peaches tried again. This time he sang louder:

"WHO WANTS TO FLY TO THE MOON?"

"I don't think your plan is working," sighed frog.

"I have another idea. Be **patient.**"

"Patient? That word again," thought frog.

Peaches tried a different song:

"Going to a ***party*** on the moon.

We have to fly there very soon.

Who wants to come along?"

"A **party**? Did you say party?

Take me right now

away to the moon,"

squeaked a little mouse

to the friendly baboon.

"Leave right now?

I don't know how.

We need some food, you see.

Bring back a treat,

something good to eat,

and I'll give you a first-class seat," said Peaches.

10 mice returned to the spaceship.

"We're ready right now,"

said ten mighty mice

wheeling in barrels

of fluffy, white rice.

Peaches and the polka dot frog

began to sing on the moss-covered log.

"Going to a *party* on the moon.

We have to leave very soon.

Who wants to come along?"

Peaches and frog waited.

They waited

and waited.

"Take me right now

away to the moon,"

buzzed a passing bee

to the friendly baboon."

"Bring back something good to eat

and I'll give you

a window seat," said Peaches.

9 spiraling bees returned to the space ship.

"We're ready to go,"

sang nine buzzing bees

flying through holes

in giant Swiss cheese.

Frog turned to his friend and asked, “Can we leave now?”

“Not yet. Be patient,” said Peaches as he checked the food supplies and looked up at the moon.

Peaches and frog returned to the moss-covered log.

“Going to a party on the moon.
Who wants to come along?”

Frog and Peaches watched and waited.
Frog wondered who would come by next.

“Can I go along too,
away to the moon?”
squawked a passing parrot
to the friendly baboon.

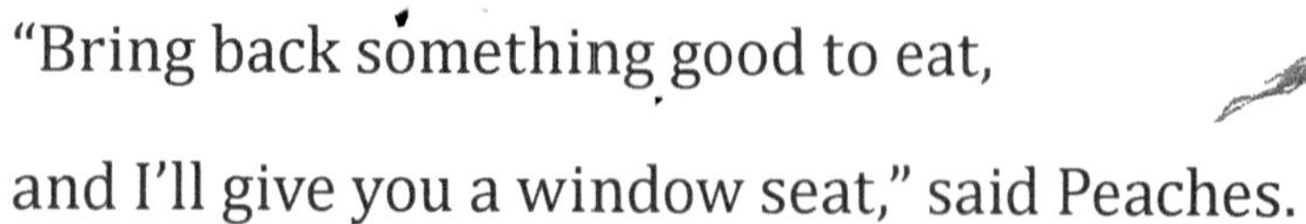

“Bring back something good to eat,
and I’ll give you a window seat,” said Peaches.

8 To the moon in June,"

sang eight pompous parrots

flying to the spaceship

with extra long carrots.

"Going to a party on the moon.

Who wants to come along?" sang Peaches and frog.

By now, all the forest animals had heard about the spaceship and the party on the moon.

"Take me right now, away to the moon,"

barked a passing poodle to the friendly baboon.

"Bring back something good to eat,

and I'll give you a window seat," said Peaches.

7 A family of seven poodles joined Peaches and frog.

"Here we are," said seven playful poodles,

tumbling and stumbling over oodles of noodles.

Once again Peaches and frog sang their song.

"Going to a party on the moon.

Who wants to come along?"

While the moon grew larger, they watched and wondered and worried.

Who would come by next?

"Ready right now," said the most bashful bunny."

Her family hopped aboard with the stickiest honey.

Bear and her family arrived at the spaceship.

"Don't forget us," groaned five **mama bears**
rolling in backwards on mounds of fresh pears.

"I think it is time to leave," said frog. "Look at all the food."

"Not yet," replied Peaches. "Not yet. Be patient."

“Take me right now, away to the moon,”

sang a slimy snail to the friendly baboon.

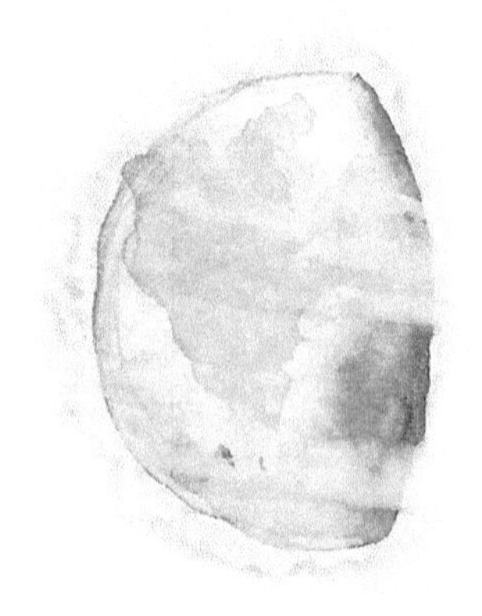

4 Snail and her family brought Peaches some food.

“Here we are,” sang the four sluggish snails,

bringing dinosaur kale with their heads not their tails.

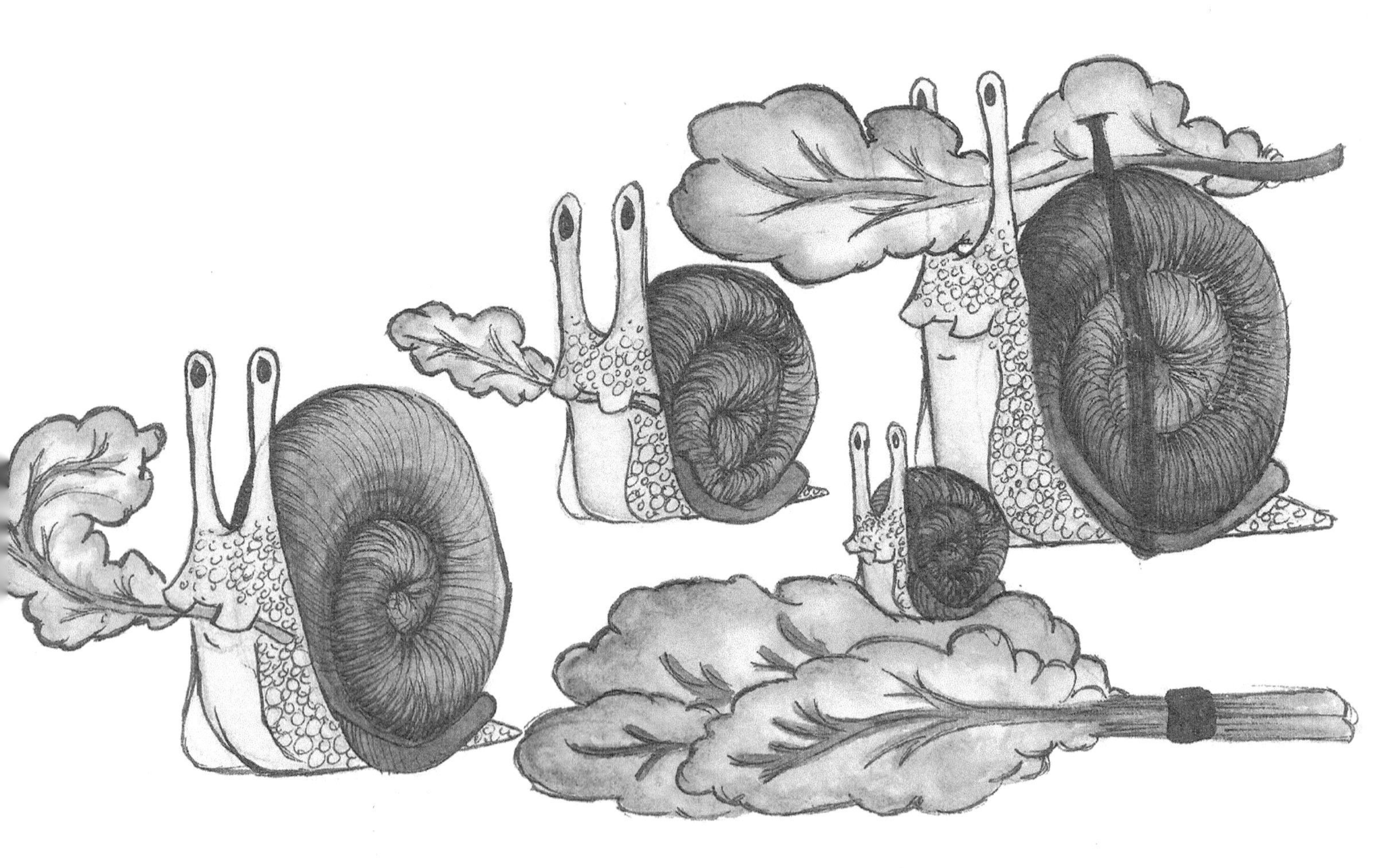

“Do we have enough food now?” asked Frog looking at the moon.

“Not yet,” said Peaches. “Not yet.”

They watched and worried and waited.

Three antelope came by next.

3 "We want to come too," sang three stately antelope saddled with bags of very large cantaloupe.

2 "We're ready to go," said two boxy fox
carrying in platters of bagels and lox.

"There is almost a full moon," said Peaches.

Frog jumped up on Peaches' shoulder. "I think the time is NOW.

Let's take off!" Frog hopped up on Peaches head.

"Almost time," replied Peaches. "Almost."

1 "Take me along too," sang Miss Kangaroo springing along, her pouch filled with stew.

Peaches thanked all his friends for the food.

"Oh, my," said Peaches. "Something important is missing and we can't leave without it. **Can you guess what it is?**

I almost forgot the **water**. Frog remembered the **bread.**

Now we are ready to leave."

"A FULL MOON AT LAST!" said frog looking up at the sky.

Suddenly frog knew what those words "be patient" meant.

Peaches locked the spaceship door.

Then he made the engines roar.

"Get ready to see

my spaceship soar!

Fasten your safety belts.

ALL SYSTEMS READY. Away to the moon!"

10 mice

9 bees

8 parrots

7 poodles

6 bunnies

5 bears

4 snail

3 antelope

2 fox and

1 kangaroo all together yelled,

"BLAST OFF!"

Above the clouds
Up, up and afar.
Into the dark.
past a shooting star.

They passed the North Star.
Next came the Big Dipper,
A bright line of lights
in the shape of a zipper.

A carpet of stars,
Some dull, some bright.
Was it still day?
Or was it now night?

Past Orion, the hunter,
Club in his hand.
Past Scorpio and Crab
looking scary but grand.

How long they traveled
I can not say,
whether forever
or a week and a day.

They saw jagged rocks,
some crushed into sand.
Then the man in the moon
pointed where they should land.

The party began, going
days without end.
Soon the man in the moon
became Peaches' best friend.

They had so much fun
Peaches decided to stay.
With a wink and a nod
and a **"hip-hip-hoo-ray."**

At the next full moon
look up at the sky,
turn on tippy toes twice
then blink your left eye.

And if you are lucky
and if it is June,
you might see Peaches
with the man in the moon.

. . . . and from that day to this,

the man in the moon

was never lonely again.

The next section is for boys and girls,
parents, teachers and librarians

HELP PEACHES CHECK HIS SUPPLIES. FILL IN THE RHYMING WORD

He thanked the mice	for bringing	*rice*
He thanked the bees	for bringing	*cheese*
He thanked the parrots	for bringing	*carrots*
He thanked the poodles	for bringing	*noodles*
He thanked the bunny	for bringing	*honey*
He thanked the bears	for bringing	*pears*
He thanked the snail	for bringing	*kale*
He thanked the antelope	for bringing	*cantaloupe*
He thanked the fox	for bringing	*lox*
He thanked kangaroo	for bringing	*stew*

QUESTIONS FOR YOU TO THINK ABOUT

. Did you guess the important food that was missing on page 25?

. Is there a food Peaches took that you have not tried? Tell about it.

. Which animal was your favorite one? Why?

. If you could travel to the moon what food would you bring? Why?

FIND THESE WORDS IN THE BOOK. TRY TO USE THEM IN A SENTENCE

"velvet" sky

"spiral" stars

"bashful" bunny

FOLLOW-UP: Find a book or a map showing stars in the evening sky.

Can you locate Scorpio, the Little Dipper, and Big Dipper and the Northern Lights?

Try drawing a picture of your favorite part of this book.

About the Author

Norma Slavit is a former Master Teacher who taught in the elementary schools of New Rochelle, New York and San Francisco. She also taught music at Hillbrook, a private school in Los Gatos, California.

A newspaper editor for the JCC Community Center in Palo Alto for over ten years, her position included being marketing and public relations manager.

Norma is a member of **SCBWI** as well as the **National League of American Pen Women.**

Many of her articles and stories have appeared in educational journals, magazines and newspapers. She has one published play to her credit, and an early story appeared in the Encyclopedia Britannica reading series.

About the illustrator

EMILY PROUGH

Emily has loved animals for as long as she can remember. She has fond memories of working at Happy Hollow Zoo in San Jose.

Throughout her high school years she studied art and qualified for

Advanced Placement Art during her senior year.

Currently, enrolled at De Anza Junior College, Emily is studying animation.

This is her first position as a book illustrator. Her ambition is to work in the animation industry.

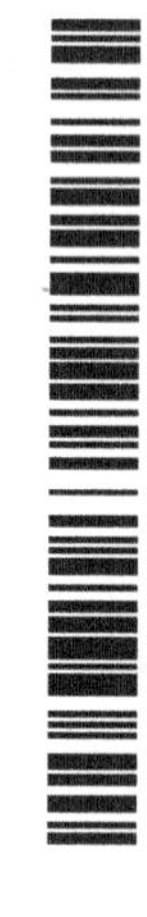

Edwards Brothers Malloy
Ann Arbor MI. USA
November 22, 2016